THE

NUMERAL

PARADOX

For requests, information, and more contact
AG Cooper III at **theamazinglilac46@gmail.com**.

Available in ebook and print.
Print ISBN: 978-1-944643-33-1
Library of Congress Control Number: 2020923744
First edition: 2020

Cover designer: Albert Cooper III

THE NUMERAL PARADOX

AG Cooper III

DEDICATION

I dedicate this book to everyone
who supported me.

CHAPTER ONE

"So, you understand what you're here for, correct?" said a middle-aged man.

"Yes," replied a woman, sitting across from him.

"Okay, your number will be nine."

"Nine?"

"Correct. Now please go to the door on your right and take a seat. I'll be in there to explain some more."

The woman got up from her chair and went to the room as directed. Opening the door, she saw eight other people seated in chairs where there was one left for her. Taking her seat, she looked around the room and noticed it was mostly empty with no windows nor color. Glancing at the crowd, she saw some were on their phones; some were waiting patiently, and some were even asleep.

"Hey, what's your number?"

The woman turned to the person beside her, who asked the question.

"It's nine," she replied.

"Cool, mine's three." said the person beside her.

"So how long do you think we'll be in here for?"

"No idea. I was the third one to show, and I've been waiting for 2 hours."

"Two hours? I hope they w-"

The door slammed open where the middle-aged man walked in, carrying a briefcase on his side.

"Welcome, everybody," he said. "My name is Detective Kyle Ryans, and all of you are here because y'all are the potential suspects for the death of Teal Robertson. As y'all may know, he was a well-known celebrity but was discovered to be a kingpin after his death. So, to prevent any of you from being targeted by his goons, you will remain here until we figure out who killed him."

"Hold up." said one of the people sitting. "What makes you think he or she or whoever will give themselves up so easily? What if the murderer doesn't confess by the end of the day?"

"I'm glad you asked," said Detective Ryans. "Each suspect will be privately questioned one by one. If we don't find the culprit by tonight, we have prepared sleeping bunks and food for the duration of our process."

Detective Ryans opened up the briefcase and pulled out stickers, he passed them to the group.

"These stickers have numbers on them. These are how you will be referred to and identified to prevent your real names from being discovered by the culprit," he said. "Now, we will start our questioning process; we do so in order. One, come with me."

One stood up and followed Detective Ryans, they started making their way back to the front.

"Hold on!" said a person labeled Four. "We got to stay here for another hour?"

"Pardon me, I forgot to mention," said Detective

Ryans. "The rest of y'all can go to the commons area, which is behind you through the hallway. There is also a vending machine if you get hungry."

The rest of the group stood up and started walking through the door behind them, where the commons area was located. The commons area was a big room consisting of bunk beds, a couch, a vending machine, and flat-screen TV in the middle. A man jumped on the couch and looked towards the group.

"Can't believe we could have been relaxing here instead of that blank-ass room." the man said.

"I know right," replied a woman.

"Well, while we're here, I guess we should go ahead and introduce ourselves. I'm Six."

"I'm Four."

"What about the rest of y'all? Don't be shy now,"

"I'm Five." said a man with glasses.

"I'm Two." said another man.

"Seven," said a woman.

"Oh, I'm Nine." said Nine.

"Hey, I'm Three!" the person beside Nine said.

"So y'all wanna watch NFL or MTV?" asked Six.

"Definitely MTV," said Four.

"Not to be a party pooper." said Two. "But I don't feel comfortable relaxing when there's a possible murderer in this room."

"I agree." said Five. "It's foolish to relax like nothing's going on."

"I mean, it's not like we got anything else to do," said Four.

"Yeah, so chill out for the time being." said Six.

"Well, y'all can have fun; I'll be sleep." yawned Seven. "Wake me up when it's my turn."

"I'll be over here reading." said Five.

"Umm...I guess I'll watch TV for now." sighed Two.

"That's the spirit, party pooper." said Six.

"You two." Four said, pointing at Nine and Three. "Come sit and watch TV with us."

"No, thanks," said Nine. "I'll be on the bed if you need me."

Nine walked over to one of the beds nearby where Seven was snoring loudly and lay down.

"How did I get myself into this mess?" she said to herself.

"So whatcha thinking about?"

Nine looked over and saw Three on the bed beside her.

"Nothing," replied Nine.

"Oh come on, you can tell me." said Three.

"It's just, I should be focusing on the new school year for my class instead of this."

"You're a school teacher?"

"It's my first year, actually."

"Cool, what do you teach?"

"Math, but specifically Algebra and AMDM."

"Wow, that's boring."

"Oh, really, what do you do then?"

"Actually, I'm unemployed, but I'm looking for a job."

"Wow. And you called my job boring."

"Believe me, unemployment is the opposite of boring."

"How so?"

"I get to party all the time, especially at Teal Robertson's place."

"So, you were friends with Teal."

"Yeah sorta, I used to work under Teal's drug operation and deliver his merchandise."

"I thought you said you were unemployed."

"Yeah, I am. Teal's dead, so now I'm unemployed."

"Oh. Okay."

"Since I was the last of my co-workers to talk to him, they think I did something to him. Now they're out to kill me. Ugh, so stressful. But enough about me, how did you know Teal."

"I tutored his son."

"Wow, that's boring."

"It's not boring. Math can mean the difference between life and death."

"That's funny."

"It's true."

Two walked over to Nine and Three.

"Three, I'm done with my interview." said Two. "He's ready for you."

"Thanks, luv," replied Three.

Three stood and left; Nine was left with her own thoughts. She remembered the day she met Teal Robertson. She just graduated from college and moved back to her parents' house. Looking for a side job, she found an ad calling for a private tutor for a 10-year-old, to which she applied. She was immediately called and hired for the job to which she would start as soon as possible. Driving to her client's residence, she was shocked to see a mansion, even more, shocked that her client was a famous celebrity, Teal Robertson. He was a nice, generous man, and she might say handsome as well. She helped his son with his work with little trouble to which she paid generously for. Every week, she would help his son, get paid, but something was off the last time she visited.

"So, you put the quotient on top of the table, understand?" said Nine.

"Yeah." said the boy.

"Since we have eight left over, how many times would three would go into eight."

"Umm.."

"Okay, I'll say it again."

"Daddy!"

Teal Robertson walked to the kitchen to where Nine was tutoring Nick, his son.

"Is Nick giving you any trouble?" asked Teal, smiling.

"Not at all, just a tad unfocused," replied Nine.

"That is my son, after all."

"Dad, you're embarrassing me," said Nick.

"Well, don't mind me, son, I'm actually here to talk to her," said Teal.

"Yes sir?" asked Nine.

"I just wanted to say thank you for helping my son get caught up with his work. And to show my appreciation, you are formally invited to the party I'm hosting tonight."

"Thank you so much, but no disrespect, I actually was going to hang out with my friends tonight."

"Well, you can bring them along too."

"We'll be there!"

Later that night, Nine and her friends were riding in her car, and they were chatting.

"I can't believe we get to party at Teal's mansion." said one of the girls.

"Me neither." said another girl. "I could kiss him and much more."

"How much more?"

"Wayyyy much more, if you know what I mean."

The girls erupted in laughter.

"Looks like we're here," said Nine. "I'll call him to open the gate."

Nine dialed Teal's number and called him.

"Hey, we're her-"

"Don't come inside. Please turn around and leave," said the man on the other end.

The phone hung up.

"Girl, did you do something to piss him off or something." asked one of the girls.

"I don't think I have," said Nine.

The phone started ringing.

"I bet that's him," said Nine as she answered the phone.

"Is this ****?"

"Yeah, that's me."

"The person you may know as Teal Robertson has been found murdered in his mansion."

"What!?"

"Also, since you are one of the last people who interacted with him today, that automatically makes you a suspect in his demise."

"Wait, no, no, no! I was only tutoring his son on long division, then he invited me to his party where I'm heading right now! There is no reason to think I would kill him!"

"So, you admit you were at his home today?"

"Yes! But that was to tutor his son; I didn't kill him!"

"No more of your excuses, you will be arrested and locked up for the rest of your l-

Nine threw her phone out the window.

"What's going on?" asked one of the girls.

"I don't know, but we have to leave now," said Nine urgently.

A police car pulled up behind them, where four officers pulled their guns towards the vehicle. Detective Ryans walked up to Nine with a smug look on his face.

"You are under arrest for the murder of Teal Roberson. Anything you say can and will be used again-"

"AHHHH!" screamed Nine.

Nine woke up from her dream and noticed she was still in bed.

"It was a dream, thank God," said Nine.

"Nah, honey." said Three. "Sounded like you had a nightmare."

"It really was. Wait, you're back. How long was I asleep for?"

"About three hours, Six is being interviewed right now. So anyways, you mind telling me what you dreamed about?"

"Nothing important."

"Oh, come on, this time it didn't sound boring."

"Just thinking about that night. What's that you're holding?"

"A screwdriver, obviously."

"Why would you bring a screwdriver?"

"You always need a screwdriver. Whether or not, it's breaking or stealing."

"Cars?"

"Yep. You can keep it."

The door slammed open again. Six entered with Detective Ryans behind him.

"Okay, so here's the deal," said Detective Ryans. "It is getting late, and I managed to interview six of y'all, which is great. So y'all will sleep here tonight, and tomorrow I will interview the rest. Then we will discuss letting whoever seems innocent go."

"You don't expect us to sleep on these cheap, tiny beds, do you?" asked Four.

"I mean, buddy enjoying herself over there, isn't she," he replied, pointing at Seven, who was still snoring loudly.

"I assume you will not be staying over here as well?" questioned Five.

"Of course not; I have a wife and daughter waiting for me at home. Make yourselves at home."

Detective Ryans left the room, then the building leaving the group to themselves. Six grabbed a blanket and laid on the couch.

"That detective was hypocritical as hell." said Six. "Old-ass doesn't know we have family at home as well?"

"Calm down." said Five. "We'll only be in here for

one night. Plus, he should spend time with his daughter."

"Okay, smartass, I guess I'll go ahead and go to sleep."

It was the dead of the night, whereas everyone was sound asleep except for one person.

"Shit, not again," said Four, who groggily woke up. "I feel like I'm about to throw up. Did that detective ever say where the bathroom was?"

Four got up and went to look for the bathroom. After what seemed too long to find, she found a door that had a bathroom symbol on it.

"About time," said Four, as she opened the door.

"AHHHH!!!!"

Some group members woke up after hearing a loud screech, while others were still sound asleep.

"Can someone tell her to shut up?" said Six groggily.

"I'll check it out," replied Two, getting up.

Two got up and searched for Four, who had made a screech just earlier and when he found her.

"AHHHH!!!!"

The other members who were asleep had now woken up after this scream, which was louder than the first.

"What the hell is going on?"" yelled Six.

"I hope it ain't serious." said One.

"I think it'll be best if all of us go check on them." said Five.

"Agreed." said One.

"You all can check it out," said Seven. "I'm going back to sleep."

The rest of the group except Seven got up and searched for Two and Four, who screamed loudly. Leading the group, Six noticed that a person was in a fetal position outside the bathroom, which he recognized as Four with Two comforting her.

"This way." said Six, who led the group to where Four and Two were at. "Y'all better have a good reason to wake me up from m- OH SHIT!"

Six saw that inside the bathroom, something so terrifying that he immediately shut the door.

"What is it?" asked Five.

"Yeah, what's happening?" chimed Three.

Six took a deep breath to regain his composure before speaking.

"Looks like there's only eight of us now." said Six.

"As in?" asked Three.

"Eight is dead."

1 3 8
4 6
9 2 6 0
7 5
1 3 8
4 6
9 2 6 0
7 5

CHAPTER TWO

The group members were sitting in the commons area waiting on Five and One, who stayed behind.

"I can't believe one of us was killed." Nine said to Three.

"You'll get used to it." Three replied.

"But how did we not notice one of us wasn't here when we arrived?" said Two.

"I'm sorry you had to see that." Six said to Four.

"It's okay, thanks for handling the situation," replied Four.

"Well, Five is doing his thing, so I'm here until you feel comfortable."

"I really appreciate that."

Three grew a smirk on their face as they looked at the two.

"Well, don't y'all look adorable together." said Three smirking.

"Three!" griped Nine.

"It's fine; actually, we're dating." said Six.

"What a coincidence," said Three with a goofy smile on their face. "I know what it's like to be committed.

It's almost like if someone could betray one another and break that commitment."

"What's that supposed to mean?" asked Six.

"You tell me, weren't you friends with Teal?"

"Are you saying that I killed Teal?"

"I'm not saying any names, but I'll be happy to say an even number."

Six stood up and walked towards Three in a threatening way.

"You better watch your mouth." said Six seriously. "I'll smack the hell out of ya if you keep talking crap."

"Please forgive them," said Nine. "They didn't mean to say that."

"It's not worth it," said Four, who stood beside Six. "Let's just come back and sit down."

"She's right." said Five, entering through the hall with One. "I have some news that might come as a surprise."

"What's that?" asked Three.

"We examined Eight's body, and we noticed that he showed no signs of blunt trauma. " said One. "So, we came to the conclusion that it was natural causes. Until we found this note."

One pulled out a folded piece of paper, which he unfolded and read it to the group.

"Say anything, incriminating, you'll pay." read One.

"We believe that the person responsible for Teal Robertson's death is also responsible for Eight's as well." said Five.

"Have you contacted the police already?" asked Nine.

"We tried, but our location is too vague for them

to track down." said One. "We'll just have to wait for Detective Ryans to arrive tomorrow."

"Are you crazy!?" exclaimed Two. "If the killer already killed one of us, then who says another one of us won't be targeted next?"

"That is because Eight probably knew who the murderer was." said Five. "That's more than enough reason to kill someone. That's why it would be best for all of us to describe our relationship to Teal Robertson to avoid suspension."

"Do we have to?" asked Four.

"Yes." replied Three. "Shouldn't be a problem, right?"

"Okay, of course," she replied.

"I'll start." said One. "I am Teal's financial advisor."

"I am Teal's cousin." said Two.

"Teal was my boss, and I used to deliver his merchandise." said Three.

"I was Teal's friend through Six," said Four.

"I am Teal's private doctor." said Five.

"I'm Teal's best friend." said Six.

"I *yawns* am...Teal's *yawns*." yawned Seven.

"I'm a tutor for Teal's son," said Nine.

"Okay, good." said One. "For our safety, I will stay up for the remainder of the night until Detective Ryans shows up. The rest of you can go back asleep."

Hours later, One got up to look around the room to make sure the others were asleep. After checking for confirmation, he went outside the commons area and straight to the interrogation room. Walking up to the desk Detective Ryans used during booking, One picked open the locked desk with a hairpin that kept his hair in place. With access to the detective's writings, One sat down and started reading them one by one. One finished reading the notes within a few minutes and placed them back into the desk as founded. Walking back to the commons area, One felt a chill run down his body. He had a hunch that he wasn't the only one awake. Stopping in the empty room, he turned around, to his relief, nobody other than he was in the hallway. Sighing out of relief, One continued on to the commons area. Suddenly he was greeted by a knife.

Elsewhere, at the break of dawn, Detective Ryans was supposed to return and finish his questioning, but things didn't go as expected.

"Be safe, honey," said Detective Ryans' wife.

"I will," replied Detective Ryans. "Hopefully, I'll find the culprit early and be home by dinner."

"That's my husband."

After exchanging a goodbye kiss, Detective Ryans, in his car, left his driveway and headed straight to the confinement center. Unbeknownst to Detective Ryans, a speeding drunk driver cruised through the empty roads without regard for safety. Turning to the right after a stop sign, Detective Ryans instantly collided with the drunk driving car, ending his journey.

Meanwhile, at the confinement center, Two, Four, Five, and Six were awake while the rest were still asleep. Two, Four, and Six were snacking and watching TV while Five excused himself to "talk" with One. While laughter was prevalent in the commons area, the empty room was filled with incredible sadness from Five looking down on One.

"Damn it." whispered Five. "Why did you insist on going?"

6 Hours Ago

The group was shocked at Six's announcement that Eight was deceased.

"But how is this possible?" asked Nine.

"Either he killed himself, or someone killed him." said Three. "I mean, spending the rest of your life in prison isn't fun, so I understand."

"That is a good point." said Two. "I think he was the one who killed Teal."

"Even if it does make him look guilty, it doesn't mean that he was the culprit." said One.

"Then why would he kill himself then?" replied Six.

"Don't forget there are a number of ways a person can die." said Five. "Natural causes, brain aneurysm, cardiac arrest, and more. As a licensed physician, I will take over from here and examine for a possible cause of death."

"I'll stay here as well, as I personally knew Eight." said One.

"If you say so." replied Six. "Come on, let's head back."

The rest of the group went back to the commons area, leaving One and Five to deal with Eight's corpse.

"I'm not as naive as the rest of them." said One. "It was clearly a murder, wasn't it?"

"The last thing we need right now is for people to panic." replied Five.

"They're going to find out sooner or later."

"Hopefully, it will be later when Detective Ryans returns and can deal with it."

"Whoever did this knew Eight had critical information about them."

"And they killed him off quickly once we were separated into the commons area. This is noticeable by how stiff his body looks, so to be already in rigor mortis means he's been dead for at least four hours."

"Whoever the murderer is isn't going to give up easily."

"I have a basic idea who it might possibly be. But before I can tell you, I need to know what happened between you and Teal the day of his death."

"Of course. I was Teal's financial advisor, and the week of his death, he started making absurd choices. He opened a third beneficiary account."

"Meaning?"

"A beneficiary account is a sum of money that is to be given to another person when the account holder dies. Sort of like a will, you might think. The first and second accounts go towards his son and aunt, but I have yet to know the beneficiary of the third account. We were discussing it early in the morning, but it was cut short when he said he was late for his doctor's appointment."

"That's surprising because I only come when he calls. He wanted me to do a check-up to which I did, and he excelled on his performance, but I gave him some pills just in case. Perhaps, he felt someone poisoned him and wanted to open another account just in case."

"That's the question, though. Who does the third account belong to?"

"Perhaps, if we ask the others how they know Teal, we could decide who the money most likely goes to?"

"Some will probably lie or give vague answers. I'll go look at the Detective's notes for a possible answer."

"You know that's a risky move because if the murderer is hell-bent on not getting caught, then you'll probably be silenced."

"Then that itself gives away who the murder is."

"Excuse me?"

"Only me, Two, Three, Four, Five and Six went to be interrogated. If you take me out and you, that means there's only 4 of 8 that couldn't have killed him. There's a 50 percent chance it's Two, Three, Four, and Six."

"That reason is flawed because there's no definite chance it wasn't. The 50 percent probability contradicts itself."

"I'll be fine; just make sure everyone stays calm."

Present

Five was still looking down on the corpse with a knife stuck in his head.

"Damn it." said Five. "If you hadn't insisted on going, then you would have still been alive."

1 3 8
4 6
9 2 6 0
7 5
1 3 8
4 6
9 2 6 0
7 5

CHAPTER THREE

In the commons area, everyone except Seven was awake either watching TV or on their phones.

"It's 1 o'clock." said Two. "Detective Ryans should have been here by now."

"I wonder if he had to stop for gas," said Nine.

"Even his old-ass shouldn't have been taking that long just for gas." said Six.

"I hope nothing bad happened." replied Two. "I really just want to go home."

"Quite in a rush, ain't ya." smirked Three. "Sounds a little suspicious."

"Three, please," whispered Nine.

"You know what seems suspicious?" said Two. "You thinking either me, Four or Six are the possible murderers. What about yourself?"

"Like I said." replied Three. "I'm not saying any names, but I'll be happy to say an even number."

"You know what?" said Six. "I'll kick your as-"

"Calm down," said Four. "I don't need you getting arrested for assault."

"If anything," replied Six. "I think Three's the one

who killed Teal. Blaming everyone else to cover your guilty ass."

"Oh, wow," said Three sarcastically. "Ain't you quite the detective. Well, seeing how I have nothing else to lose, I'll tell my sequence of events."

6 Days Ago

"Ding-dong." said Three, pushing the button to the gate.

"Password?" asked the gate intercom."

"DD, 2689."

The gate opened to Teal Robertson's mansion, where Three started walking towards the massive mansion on foot. They rang the doorbell, where it was opened by Teal's housekeeper.

"Ah, come in; Mr. Teal will see you in the parlour." said the housekeeper.

"Thanks luv," said Three.

Three slid a one-dollar bill into the housekeeper's pocket.

"Hey, Mr. Bossman!" said Three, walking down to the parlor room.

"Shut the door," said Teal Robertson. "This is urgent."

"Of course, of course. What's the matter?"

"I'm going to die tonight."

"Wait, you're thinking about killing yourself, are ya?

"Of course not. I just know I'm going to die tonight."

"Well, shouldn't ya cancel the party and go to the doctor?"

"I already called the doctor earlier and said I don't

have much longer to live."

"So whatcha' need me to do?

"During the party tonight, I want you to remove every trace of cocaine. This will prevent my legacy from being tainted."

"So, what about your son?"

"I already set things up for him to get half of my estate, my aunt as well, and I just opened up one more for-"

"Sorry to interrupt, Master Teal." said the housekeeper who opened the door. "Nick's tutor has arrived."

"We'll finish this later," Teal said to Three.

Present

"I think I understand." said Two. "The third beneficiary account belongs to one of us. Because if the account went to the murderer, then that's why he was killed."

"Bingo!" remarked Three.

"I did the math in my head," said Nine. "Since there are currently eight of us, that means there's a 12.5 percent chance the account went to us."

"Considering he already had an account for my mom, I doubt the other one was for me." said Two.

"Me and Teal's relationship is somewhat business casual." said Three.

"Plus, he already gave me some money before he passed." said Six. "Said it was an apology, but I don't know for what."

"But what about your boo?"

"He only met Four a few times, dumbass."

"Just making sure."

"Nine, I've been meaning to ask you something." said Two.

"About what?" replied Nine.

"Teal talked about you a few times before he passed. How were you affiliated with him?"

"He's my boss. I tell him about his son's progress."

"Enough about my weird cousin. What I'm asking is, were you and Teal in a relationship?"

"Absolutely not. He's my boss."

"You were invited to his party, weren't you? That means you must've been pretty close."

"Then, he later told me not to come for some reason."

"So, you had his phone number, didn't you?"

"Chill out, Two." said Three.

"Bruh, if Teal wanted a relationship, he would've hired some hoes." said Six. "No offense, Nine, but I don't believe Teal would settle for you."

"Oh, okay," said Nine, taking it offensively.

"You didn't have to say that." said Three.

"Hey, I said no offense." replied Six. "I just would find it shocking if Teal actually settled for Nine."

"If you ask me, I find it shocking that Four would settle for you." Three quipped to Six.

"That's it." replied Six, who stood up.

Walking towards Three, Six delivered a pimp slap to the face. A few seconds later, Six was slapped back by Three, starting a brawl between the two. Soon, the fight between the two was stopped by Nine and Four, who restrained Three and by Two, who put Six in a chokehold.

"Enough!" yelled Five, entering through the hallway. "I overheard bits of your conversation, including the third beneficiary account Teal opened up. Against my advice, One broke into the detective's documents, where he must have learned who the account goes to. And because of that, he was slain."

The group was shocked and immediately many side conversations erupted, which was quickly ended by Five.

"It's 3:30. Where the hell is Detective Ryans?" said Six.

"You haven't heard the news?" said Five.

"What news?" asked Two.

"Concerning Detective Ryans." replied Five.

"No, because this ass here was starting fights." said Six, pointing at Three.

"Oh, boy." sighed Five.

"Oh no!" screamed Four, who was looking at her phone.

"What's wrong?" asked Six.

"Take a look at this," she replied.

Six looked over at Four's phone to see what she saw that made her react like that. After seeing what happened on Four's phone, Six facepalmed and started murmuring profanities. Seeing Six's reaction, Two, Three, and Nine went and looked at Four's phone as well. Four's phone showed a recently posted news video regarding Detective Ryans.

"A shocking scene just happened this morning where district police detective, Kyle Ryans Jr., was struck by a drunk driver at over 100 miles per hour. Kyle Ryans was transported to the local hospital ICU, where he is currently being prepared for surgery. Our thoughts and prayers are with Detective Ryans. We'll have more information on his status later this evening."

"Just great," said Two, upset. "Now, we're stuck in here with a serial killer."

"The police should realize eventually that we're still here," said Nine.

"They better." said Six.

"I doubt they'll come, at least not until tomorrow." said Five.

"I can't do one more night." said Two.

"Yeah, what if one more of us dies?" asked Nine.

"This is what we will do." said Five.

Five held up a hairpin with his hand to the group.

"This is the hairpin that One used to access Detective Ryan's documents." said Five. "The murderer would have gotten this if they needed the documents. That suggests that One was killed to prevent a secret from getting out."

"Like being the holder of the third beneficiary account?" questioned Nine.

"Exactly." replied Five. "As of now, I will place us on complete lockdown. No one is allowed to leave the commons area until the police arrive."

"What about our bathroom needs?" asked Four.

"Then they will be accompanied by another person as well." answered Five. "Does anyone object to this?"

"Nope." said Three.

"Not at all," said Nine.

"Let's just get this over with." said Six.

"Agreed." said Two.

"Then it's settled." responded Five. "As of now, we are on complete lockdown. You all are dismissed, but Four, I would like to talk to you in private."

"What's wrong." asked Six.

"Actually, I need to talk to you two privately." replied Five. "But, I would like to talk with Four before you."

"Hold on, don't tell me you think Four killed Teal."

"I'm just asking questions, calm down."

"It's okay." Four said to Six. "Let's go ahead and do this, and we'll be done faster."

"Okay, as long you're fine with it." replied Six.

"Great." said Five. "Now, follow me."

Five and Four walked through the hallway, passing One's corpse all the way to the interrogation room on the opposite side of where they came. Five pulled a chair from the detective's desk, shutting the door behind them.

"Four, you were the one who discovered Eight, correct?" asked Five.

"Yes," replied Four.

"I noticed you haven't been talking as much since that moment. I don't think you're capable of killing Teal Robertson. I have a feeling it might have been Six."

"I see."

"Are you okay with potentially giving your boyfriend up, knowing that he could end up spending the rest of his life in prison?

"Yes."

"But you and Six were at his party the night he died, correct?"

"Yes."

"Do you mind telling your experience that night?"

27

"Okay, Me and Six was at Teal's party by 7 o'clock, where we were just having fun. Then suddenly Six excused himself to talk to Teal, leaving me by myself. Then later, Six came out with a bag of money, which he said he got from Teal. We were still partying until the housekeeper screamed that Teal was dead. Mostly everybody evacuated except us and a few others that talked to the police."

"Ah, I see. When Six went to talk to Teal, he was murdered, and that was where Six got the money from?"

"Correct."

"That's all I wanted to know. Thank you. You must promise not to tell Six about anything we discussed in here, understand?"

"Of course, I promise."

"Before you go, I need to tell you something important."

"What's that?"

"I am going to hide the hairpin inside One's pants. After I question Six, I will also tell him as well. This is a bait trap; if the hairpin inside One's pants is gone by tomorrow, that means Six without a doubt killed One and possibly Teal as well. It's extremely vital that this stays between us, understand?"

"Yes, I promise."

"Good, you can leave and tell Six to come here."

Four left the room back to the commons area, where Six was waiting for her.

"He said he's ready for you." Four said to Six.

"Alright, babe." replied Six walking off.

Four went to sit down on the couch, where Three and

Nine were seated.

"Whatcha talked about?" asked Three.

"He just asked me about the night Teal died," replied Four.

"Four, did he accuse you of being the murderer?" asked Nine.

"No, but sighs, I gave up my boyfriend."

"Six is the murderer?" exclaimed Two.

"What did I say? smiled Three. "I was right; it was an even number that killed Teal."

"No way. They've known each other since college; it doesn't make no sense."

"Honey, a lot of stuff doesn't make sense."

"Just please don't tell him about this," begged Four. "He'll be really upset with me."

"We understand," replied Nine. "Six won't know about this."

A few minutes later, Six and Five returned to the commons area. Six noticed he was getting weird looks from some of the others but thought nothing more of them. As per Five's lockdown method, the couch was moved in front of the entrance, blocking the way. But that didn't stop one person from quietly climbing over the sofa in search of the hairpin located on One.

The next day, Five gathered the whole group, even Seven, who was still sleepy. Five led the rest to One's corpse, moving the couch out the way, where the answer to the murderer was.

Three spoke up, "So now we're here, can we hurry up and see who the murderer is?"

"Of course." replied Five. "But first, we need to examine the body and see if the evidence is still there."

"But who would be stupid to remove the hairpin." said Six.

"One apparently that was heartless enough to kill Teal apparently." spoke up Two.

"Don't tell me you think I killed Teal too."

"Gentleman, hold on." said Five, examining One's body.

Five held up One's head, reaching his hand underneath and grabbing a hairpin to which he showed the group.

"See, I told you nobody would give themselves up so stupidly." said Six.

"Hold on," said Four. "You told me that the hairpin was in his pockets."

"I did." replied Five. "I hid it in two different spots, but I gave you both different locations. But see, I found the hairpin where I told Six, but not where I told you."

"A bait trap," said Nine. "That means.."

"Four." pointed Five. "You are the murderer."

CHAPTER FOUR

"Four." said Six. "Please tell me you're not a killer."

"I'm so sorry." sobbed Four.

"Oh my god."

"But that's not all." said Five. "While you defended her, she gave you up, stating you killed him."

"Damn, that's cold." quipped Three.

"Four, you bitch!" screamed Six.

"I'm sorry." sobbed Four. "But I didn't kill Teal. I only killed One."

"Like that makes everything better!"

"Eight and One was killed because they knew the third beneficiary account holder," said Nine. "So that means."

"The account goes to you." finished Five.

"Bingo." said Three.

"Wait, you cheated on me." asked Six.

"Hold on." interrupted Two. "I didn't tell anybody this because I didn't think it would be useful. When my mother was granted access to her account, they had to ID her because the bank said something about beneficiaries being only granted to family members."

"And besides Two, none of us are related to Teal," said Nine.

"So why would Four kill them if she wasn't the account holder?" asked Six.

"Like you said, family members." said Five. "She obviously has a big secret if she would kill to prevent it from coming out."

"But she and Teal ain't related!" exclaimed Six.

"Idiot." said Three. "Have you not figured it out?"

"Shut up!" yelled Six. "Four, if you and Teal were... hold on...Teal gave me money as an apology so... don't tell me... Four, are you?"

Four looked down and rubbed her stomach, answering his question. Six held his hands in disbelief as he realized the truth about the two people he considered his closest friends.

"Four, how long have you known you were pregnant?"

"A week before his death," replied Four.

"Five, thank you for showing me the people I thought were my best buddies were actually cheating f****," said Six. "As for the rest of you, I'm going to sleep, don't disturb me, or I will beat the hell out of y'all."

"I'm sorry." sobbed Four.

"You know what." Six replied. "You can go to hell for all I care, probably where Teal is at too."

Six walked off, muttering profanities along the way.

"So... what now?" said Three.

"Getting the hell out of here, that's what." replied Two.

"You remember the doors are locked from the outside?" said Five.

"I don't care; I'm not staying another night. What about the rest of y'all?"

"I guess I'll help," replied Nine.

"If she doing it, I guess I am too." said Three.

"I'm *yawns* kinda tired," said Seven. "I'm going back to bed."

"I see." said Five, pushing his glasses. "I'll deal with Four while y'all search for an alternate exit."

Two, Three, and Nine spread out around the building, looking for an escape method for a few hours, to no avail.

"I swear the police are so useless." said Three. "Don't know why that detective had to put us in the middle of nowhere."

"To protect us, but I wonder if this was a mistake," replied Nine.

"What do you mean?" asked Two.

"It's just, why are there only nine of us here when there were more people at Teal's party?"

"Beats me."

"Because everyone who was there wasn't as close to him as the nine of us." said Five walking through the door. "The purpose of this wasn't just to protect us, but to make sure that anyone who was connected to Teal had important information. That's why people like you and me were selected because we would have likely known of Teal's illegal operations."

"I had no idea of Teal's drug dealings until he died," said Nine.

"Unfortunately, I never had that privilege. Three, I heard you were working under Teal."

"Sounds about right." replied Three.

"Then surely it doesn't make sense why you're the only one of his crew to be in this confinement center."

"Truth is, I was the one who exposed Teal's operation."

"What!" exclaimed Nine.

"It's a long-ass story."

A Week Ago

"It was on the night of Teal's party; I was in the basement with my co-workers packing the merchandise in the truck where it was to be moved elsewhere. The last I heard of Teal was when he excused himself to give some money to his friend after he got his girlfriend preggers.

"You're talking about Six and Four, right?" asked Nine.

"Yes, now, don't interrupt me. Back to the story, the truck was ready to move, but the fence was blocked. So I went upstairs to the party to get Teal, but that was when the housekeeper screamed like hell. Then, I heroically went to see what the fuss was about. Well shit, Teal was dead on the floor like a bug. The party went to hell that quick.

People were rushing out of there, running through the fence with their cars, and when I went back to the basement, my co-workers left me behind. I had no car, so I couldn't escape, and plus the cops were there in like, two minutes. The guys didn't do a good job because there were still bags of cocaine in the basement, not to mention it was on my clothes too. Long story short, I was arrested. I was so pissed at my co-workers that I gave every one of them up, and they didn't like that. After bailing out, I barely survived three attempts on my life. So, I went to Detective Ryans, where he offered protection and a lesser sentence in exchange to stand in court. And here we are."

Present

"I was expecting something new and important." said Two.

"Agreed, we already know about the housekeeper finding the body and cocaine." said Five.

"Ugh, y'all so ungrateful," whined Three.

"What happened to the housekeeper?" asked Nine.

"Apparently, she was so traumatized that she got hooked on sleeping pills or something."

"Any chance it might have been her who killed Teal?" asked Five.

"Naw! She couldn't hurt a butterfly, let alone kill a grown man."

"Teal was healthy enough for me to pass off when I checked him out earlier, so I doubt that as well."

"You checked off Teal as healthy?"

"Yes, is there something wrong?"

"First, there's something I need to tell you about?" Nine said to Three. "During that period of time before Teal's death when I was waiting at the gate with my friends, I called him. He told me to turn around and leave in an urgent manner, which I did. I think it might be possible that he was struggling before he died."

"That confirms the killer had to be at the party." said Five.

"Exactly. If we do the math, we can confirm that Two, Three, Four, and Six were at the party. I don't know about Seven or Eight, so we'll exclude them along with Three. I conclude there's a 33% percent chance of the murderer being Two, Four or Six."

"Whoa!" exclaimed Two. "That's my cousin; why would I kill him?"

"Who knows." shrugged Three.

"I can honestly say, I didn't kill him." insisted Two. "Hell, it might as well have been Four. After all, she did kill One and possibly Eight for all we know."

"Oh yeah, Doc, what did you do with Four?"

"I used the spare handcuffs in Detective Ryans' desk to chain her to the pole in the blank room." replied Five.

"Does he have some Febreeze or something? It's starting to smell like ass in here."

"It seems like the corpses finally started decomposing."

"Ugh, someone open the vents or something."

"That's it," exclaimed Nine.

"What's it?" asked Two.

Nine pointed up the ceiling where there is an air vent attached.

"Genius!" exclaimed Five. "If one of us can climb the vents, then they could go get help and set us free."

"Nine, I knew you were smart!" cheered Three.

"Thank God!" said Two. "I'll go tell the others."

"Go ahead." said Five. "Nine and Three, help me stack these chairs, would you?"

Two exited the interrogation room as the rest of the group were stacking the chairs; he came across an unpredictable surprise.

"Oh shit!" yelled Two.

"Oh, Lord, please don't let this be." muttered Five.

Exiting out the door, Five saw what caught Two's attention. Four, still chained to the pole, was lying on the floor unconscious. Nine and Three came out as well as saw the shocking event. Five hurriedly went to Four and checked on her while removing the handcuffs.

"Her heart's not beating!" yelled Five. "I'll start compressions."

"I'll help you," said Nine. "I took a CPR class before I could get my teaching license."

"Okay, we'll switch out every 30 seconds."

As Five and Nine started compressions on Four, Three, and Two were both thinking the same thing.

"I think it's obvious who did this." said Three.

"Let's pay him a visit."

Two and Three went to the commons area, which was trashed, but Six and Seven seemed to be asleep.

"Six, wake up man." said Two as he shook Six.

"What did I say about waking me up?" murmured Six.

"Did you make Four go unconscious?"

"Of course not, but she deserved it."

"So, you admit it was it you." said Three.

"No, I didn't."

"But you said she deserved it, though. I can see why you could have. She left you for a richer, handsomer friend. You must've been really jealous."

"Three, enough man." ushered Two.

"Let me finish, you knew she was cheating on you from the beginning; why else would you take a random bag of money as an apology if you didn't know. I think, no, I know you killed Teal."

"For the last time. I. Did. Not. Kill. Anyone." Six said sternly.

"He's right." said a woman.

Seven stood up and walked towards Two, Three, and Five.

"Five," said Seven. "The reason why Three kept accusing you and Four is because they knew about the affair."

"Duh." said Three.

"Hush. Come here."

Seven whispered into Six's ear, which made him furious. In the other room, Five and Nine were still continuing compressions on Four until...

coughs

"She's breathing!" exclaimed Five.

"Four, are you alright?" asked Nine.

"She still seems to be unconscious, but she's breathing. Let's give her some time to rest, then we'll ask her what happened."

"Okay."

CRASH

"What in the world?" questioned Five.

Three was thrown onto the floor in the blank room where Four, Five, and Nine were at.

"Three, what happened!?" asked Nine.

"I pissed off Six, so now he's coming after me." replied Three, labored.

"I'd be lying if I say I didn't see this coming." said Five. "You always run your month."

"Okay, smartass. But Seven said something to him that made him attack me."

"Three!!"

Six was in the hallway trying to rush towards Three but was being held back by Two semi-successfully.

"Run!" yelled Two.

Three ran back to the interrogation room along with Five and Nine, who dragged Four along. Slamming the door, Three and Five moved the table in front of the door. Six eventually broke Two's restraint on him and started banging on the door, trying to enter. Two who ran towards Six, trying to place him in a chokehold as previously. But Six was built like a linebacker and pissed off, it became a near-impossible task for Two to pull off.

"Calm down!" yelled Two.

"Two, stop! This is between me and that bastard!" replied Six.

"They found a way out! If you kill Three, then you'll go to jail!"

"I don't give a damn!"

"I know they're annoying as hell, but still! I won't let you kill Three!"

"Three killed Teal!"

"What?"

"That's why that bastard kept trying to frame me."

"Exactly," said Seven, entering the room. "I was

there when the housekeeper yelled that Teal's dead. But, I saw a person exiting the room carrying money. Besides, they worked for Teal, so it makes sense."

Two relaxed Six from his grip as he pondered the situation.

"Oh, man." said Two. "How did I not see this coming?"

"Now, you understand." said Six.

"Don't feel bad," said Seven. "Everyone was lying about something, including the affair. But I did teach the girl a lesson while she was chained."

"Can't lie and say I'm not a bit satisfied. I'm still pissed at Teal, but I guess he didn't deserve to die. I say, let's bring him some justice."

"Okay." said Two. "Count me in."

Next door in the interrogation room, Three, Six, and Nine were still trying to reach the vents but with little success. Then the door busted open, with Two, Six, and Seven entering.

"We want Three." said Two.

"What did Seven tell you?" asked Three.

"That you killed Teal, obviously. But she said you were there after the party and took some money as well. You were a part of Teal's crew, and you snitched on his drug operation."

"So, you tried to frame me and Four." said Six. "You knew of Teal's affair and kept quiet until Five told me. Before that, I didn't know why Teal gave me apology money. Now we know your ass is guilty."

"Why the hell would you believe Seven?" exclaimed Three. "Bitch been sleeping this whole time until now.

Does she have any proof of what she's saying?"

"I do," said Seven.

Seven pulled off her hair which was a wig, and then her sunglasses as well.

"Because I am Teal's housekeeper."

"The housekeeper?!" exclaimed Nine.

"Yes, that's me." answered Seven.

"I thought you went crazy and got hooked on sleeping pills." said Three.

"Crazy, no, but taking sleeping pills, yes."

"You had me fooled too." said Two.

"But why were you in disguise?" asked Five.

"Because I needed to protect myself. As the one who found Teal's body, some people would think I killed him."

"That actually does makes sense."

"So there's your proof." said Six. "Now, get your ass over here."

"I tipped you good, and this is how you repay me?" Three said to Seven.

"Wait, Three, did you actually kill Teal?" asked Nine.

"Hell no! Yes, I snitched on his drug operation. Yes, I knew about the affair. But I swear I would never kill Teal. He respected me for who I am. He gave me a job, paid me well. No, I did not kill Teal! Plus, he was already dead when you found him, and I was still walking up from the basement. Who says you didn't kill him?"

"Please," smirked Seven. "I respect him too much to do that. Plus, a small woman like me against a big man. Do you know how stupid you sound?"

"Plus, she did said she saw a man walking out with

money." said Two.

"People, let's relax," said Five. "He could have been poisoned or died of natural causes."

"Five, I respect you for being Teal's doctor and giving him medicine." said Seven. "Nine, I respect you for tutoring his son. Please hand over Three to us, or we will do it by force."

"I don't believe Three was the murderer," said Nine.

"Neither do I," said Five.

"I'm sorry then," said Two.

"I'm not." said Six taking off his shirt.

Five attempted to push the door, but Six effortlessly pushed though. Three tried to avoid Six by running around the table that was pushed out the way. Six was pushed by Five, who was then attacked by Two. But Nine smacked Two with a chair, letting off. Seven ran at Nine attacking her, which was stopped by Three, who punched Seven. The ongoing brawl between Two, Six, and Seven vs. Three, Five, and Nine was a brutal one. Not a single person was unharmed. After a while, Three managed to escape outside the room with Five and Nine shortly behind and ran to the bathroom where Eight's corpse was still lying. Slamming and locking the door, Three, Five, and Nine heard the others banging on the door, trying to get in.

"God, it stinks in here." said Three.

"Just shut up and focus!" replied Five. "Where's the vent?"

"Up there," said Nine, pointing to the ceiling.

"Three, help me lift her up."

Three and Five lifted Nine up from her shoes. She

managed to get a grip and remove the cover from the air vent. Dropping the cover, she jumped and climbed up the vent.

"I'm in!" said Nine.

"Good!" replied Five. "Now remember, the vents should lead to the entrance where you can climb down after removing the cover like here. Afterwards, hurry and get help as soon as possible."

"I got you!" replied Nine as she started leaving.

Three and Five were now by themselves locked in the cramped bathroom. It doesn't help that Two, Six, and Seven were outside the door either.

"This is bad." said Five.

"Ehh, life happens." replied Three.

"So, according to Seven, she found Teal dead before anyone else."

"Yeah, I think someone poisoned him."

"So it seems."

"You are Teal's personal doctor, correct?"

"Correct."

"I've been meaning to ask you, Doc, were you the same doctor who told Teal he was dying?"

"You see-,"

"Answer the question. You said you were Teal's private doctor, yet you told us that he was healthy at the first meeting. But earlier, Teal told me the opposite, and even Seven said he was taking medicine. Tell me, did you do something?"

"Yes."

"What did you do?"

"I got my revenge."

1 3 8

4

6

9 2 6 0

7 5

1 3 8

4 6

9 2 6 0

7 5

CHAPTER
FIVE

"Life was good; I had a house, a good-paying job, and a beautiful daughter. Like I said, life was good. I prided myself in my work; it was only with much dedication, which led me to having enough money to give my daughter the life she deserves. The life that I never got to have. My daughter was a joy; even though my wife departed from this earth, she still left a beautiful girl that I promised to protect until I die. It wasn't easy being a single father, I'll tell you that. It definitely ain't easy raising a little girl, but I made it work. She was a good student, All A's, perfect attendance, and had a pretty smile.

One day, she came home with great news. She found a boyfriend and his name was Teal Robertson. He seemed like a nice, respectful young man, someone I would gladly allow to date my daughter. Before I knew it, he became my son-in-law, and my daughter was no longer a little girl. They eventually had a son, and I became a grandfather. Life was good.

I decided to pay them a visit and found out then Teal was dealing drugs. This led to a shouting match between me and him privately. I threatened him with going to the police if he didn't stop, and he agreed to that condition.

But then, one day, my little girl departed from this world as well. Her cause of death? Drug overdose. I beat that man half to death with my own hands and disowned him. He kept saying he was remorseful and tried to win me back with money and gifts. But he took away my greatest gift, that nothing can replace.

He eventually did manage to win me back with a large sum of money, but not as his father- in-law, but as a private doctor. I wanted to hurt him, so I lied and told him he was dying and prescribed a prescription for him. But I didn't know he would actually die later that night. My grandson has no parents because of me, one for not protecting her and the other for killing him. I'm the reason life isn't good for him right now."

Present

"Damn." said Three wiping their eyes. "I didn't realize you went through that. What did you plan on doing after all this?"

"I planned on writing my will, giving everything to my grandson. Then hang myself shortly after."

"That's some bullshit, old man."

"Excuse me?"

"You feel responsible for the death of your grandson's parents, so you gon' make him lose his grandfather as well?"

"I haven't seen him in five years."

"I don't give a damn. After all this, you are going to

make it up to him. You raise him as his dad like with your daughter, because that was her greatest gift to you."

Five was taken aback from that statement as if he was genuinely blind until now.

"I needed to hear that, thank you."

"No problem, Doc."

"Though I probably won't be able to, since I'll be in jail for killing Teal."

"Don't worry about that, I'll take your place."

"No, you don't need to do that."

"I'm already looking at 1-3 years in jail; what's ten more years?

"Don't be foolish!"

"Too bad, I already am!"

The conversation was stopped instantly once they heard the door locks break.

"Quick, move the dead body to the door!" said Five.

"What's that supposed to do?" questioned Three.

"It'll hold them off. Corpses are harder to move since their bodies stiffen after death. Now hurry!"

Elsewhere, Nine managed to find the nearest exit point to which she kicked open. The exit led outside. She climbed out.

"Finally," said Nine relieved. "Oh, God."

Nine looked around and realized she was outside but on top of the confinement center. Nine walked around to look for an emergency staircase or a ladder.

"Okay, I see this is going to be difficult."

Nine took off her jacket and tied it around her waist.

"This looks to be at least 20 feet from the ground.

Honestly, I'll need a drink after this."

Nine took a few steps back, then she ran and jumped from the building onto one of the cars. She flopped like a fish; needless to say, she was injured, but she got up and walked to the blaring car. Then she remembered something important Three said and pulled out a screwdriver from her pocket.

"You always would need a screwdriver. Whether or not, it's for breaking or stealing."

"Three, I owe you one," said Nine.

Nine pulled out the screwdriver and jammed the keyhole unlocking it. Taking it out, she then jammed it into the ignition, cranking it up. She was literally in the middle of nowhere, Nine sped off, rushing to the nearest police station. Inside, the rest of the group were terrorized by the gang of Six, Two, and Seven.

"Shit, this is bad." Three said. "What the hell should I do? What would the others think?"

Three remembered what Nine said earlier.

Math can mean the difference between life and death.

"No the hell it doesn't!"

"Are you talking to yourself?" said Five.

"Yeah,"

The door was burst open by Six, who proceeded to punch Three in the face several times. As futile Three tried to fight back, he simply couldn't as Six began to strangle him. Fading out of consciousness, Three passed out. Six's hold around Three's neck was released when Five smashed the toilet tank cover over his head. Two and Seven went after Five and starting pushing and stomping on him. Within a few seconds, he grabbed Seven's leg and knocked her towards Two, giving him time to run. Running back towards the commons area, Five immediately pushed the sofa against the door, blocking the entry. Collapsing on the floor to take a breath, Five was depleted. Even a minute later, when he heard the sofa being moved, he was simply too tired to move. Two and Seven entered the area with an intent to kill, and Five accepted his fate until...

"Police freeze!"

Five turned around to see police storming the building. Holding his hands up, Five sighed out of relief that this nightmare was finally over.

"Breaking news, nine suspects of celebrity Teal Robertson's death were trapped in a terrifying situation. The suspects were sent to a confinement center for protection while being interrogated under Detective Kyle Ryans, who was in a car crash earlier this week. For protection, the suspects' names shall not be named and referred to by the number assigned to them. The suspects were trapped for almost three days until one of them, Nine, managed to escape while spraining her ankle and drove to the police. Shortly afterward, the police arrived at the confinement center along with paramedics.

This might seem like a happy ending, but sadly it wasn't. There were 4 confirmed fatalities and 6 injured. One and Eight were killed early on after Detective Ryans' accident. One allegedly was killed by Four, as it was revealed he knew she was pregnant with Teal's child. Eight's murderer is still unknown. An investigation is still ongoing. Six was killed in self-defense as he allegedly attacked the group along with Two and Seven. Four was attacked afterwards, apparently as revenge. Unfortunately, her child was the fourth fatality. She will be released to the authorities after being dismissed from the hospital to plead guilty to second-degree murder. The rest of the suspects except for Three and Four had been released from the hospital. Two and Seven were arrested on attempted murder charges that were lowered to aggravated assault. The police station is facing harsh criticism for their unawareness of the situation. We will have more on this story later as it develops."

The news station was shut off by Three, who was resting on the hospital bed.

"Well ain't that some shit." wheezed Three.

"The fact you're alive is," replied Nine. "Your throat was literally crushed."

"It takes more than that to kill me."

"Honestly, I hope you don't go starting fights again."

"And I hope you don't go jumping off buildings again."

"I just can't with you."

"I know."

Three and Nine were in the hospital room where Three was lying on the bed with a neck collar while Nine only had a leg cast.

"It seems like you two are lively this morning."

Walking into the room was Five and Nicky, who had flowers and chocolates.

"Doc?" Three said, surprised.

"Nicky!" exclaimed Nine.

"I heard you jumped off a building to escape," said Nicky. "That's so cool."

"Nick!" exclaimed Five.

"Are these chocolates for us?" asked Three.

"Actually they're for Nine. I thought you died."

"Come on, I worked in a drug gang. I've been through worse."

"You sure are lucky to be alive."

"All thanks to you, and Nine."

"Of course," said Nine.

"You were Dad's old friend?" asked Nicky.

"Something like that." replied Three.

"So, he really was dealing drugs?"

"It wasn't bad or just. Yes, but he, he just wanted to support his family. But he made the wrong choices and paid for it. Just know, you don't have to make the same choices he did. Use your money to make good decisions; however you like. That's all it comes down to."

"Yes sir. Yes ma'am?"

"And that applies to me too," said Five. "It seems we both made bad decisions and paid for it. I will make up for it by raising my grandson the best I can."

"Granddad, I'm 10. I'm grown."

"Haha." laughed Nine. "Wait until you get to college."

"Or start paying taxes." said Three.

"And start having back pains." said Five.

"Not that old!" said Nicky.

"Hahaha." laughed everyone else.

"Nine, would you still be interested in being Nicky's

tutor for the upcoming school year?" asked Five.

"I'm actually going to start teaching at the middle school," said Nine. "I'm sorry, but I can't."

"Which middle school?"

"Whitewood Middle School."

"I guess that's the school he'll enroll in."

"Wow, you don't have to do that."

"It's for the best, anyone else as his teacher, and he would undoubtedly fail math."

"Granddad!" said Nicky. "You didn't have to say that."

"Hehe. I guess I'll see you next month," said Nine.

"I look forward to it!"

"As for you Three, any news for what's to happen?" asked Five.

"The plea deal I took from Detective Ryans was supposed to shorten my sentence to 1-3 years. But since I'm taking the fall for the crime, I could be looking at 20 years."

"When I gave my account of what happened to the police, I did not mention any of the things I told you. As far as I know, they are still looking for the killer."

"Killer?" questioned Nicky. "For the people in the facility, you was at?"

"Um, yes," answered Five.

"Great, Doc." said Three sarcastically. "I'm still looking at 3 years in jail."

"I can buy you out of jail if you want me to," said Nicky.

"Hold up." said Three. "Whatcha mean?"

"Dad used to be friends with the judges. I'll just give

them money not to arrest you."

"Now Nicky, we can't start bribing people," said Five.

"Why? Dad used to do it. Plus, I'm using my money to make good choices."

"You don't have to spend that much money on me." said Three.

"It's fine. I have enough to buy the whole prison if I wanted."

"Well shit," Three smiled. "I guess I owe you one. Doc, Nine, we need to go get drinks after I get out."

"Agreed," said Nine.

"Of course, let's end this experience on a good note." said Five.

"Hold on." said a woman.

The group turned around to see Detective Ryans walking through the door.

"Detective Ryans?" said Nine.

"Yes, I need to talk to you, Three and Five privately," replied Detective Ryans.

"Nicky, would you step out for a minute?" asked Five, to which he obliged.

Closing the door behind him, Detective Ryans, who was still in a hospital gown, sat on a chair.

"I am sorry, y'all had to go through that," said Detective Ryans.

"You had a car crash," said Nine. "You don't have to apologize."

"To tell the truth, the reason I am here is… you can bring her in."

The door opened, where a police officer escorted

Seven into the room handcuffed.

"She will tell you," said Detective Ryans.

"About what?" asked Five.

"How Teal actually died."

CHAPTER ZERO
(FINAL CHAPTER)

"When the party started, I noticed Teal was stressed out. I tried to calm him down, but he still couldn't relax. He told me about how his doctor told him he was dying, and he found out he got his friend's girlfriend pregnant. Not to mention, he was trying to clear all evidence of drugs before his death. The pills made him relax somewhat, but he was still hesitant. He went to give his friend some money but didn't tell him about the affair. But when he came back, it turned for the worst."

"Teal, what's wrong?" I asked.

"Everything!" exclaimed Teal. "I feel like my heart is about to explode."

"Have you tried the pills?"

"Yes!"

"Then the phone rang to show Nicky's tutor was calling."

"Don't come inside. Please turn around and leave." Teal said, answering the phone.

"Teal, we need to go to the hospital," I said.

"Not yet; I need to make sure all the evidence is

gone. Tell them to go ahead and leave."

"The drug truck?"

"Yes!"

"I went down to the basement and told them to go and leave immediately. As I ran back up to his room, I saw he was slumped over on the bed, coughing blood."

"Teal!" I screamed.

"Don't call nobody." Teal pleaded. "If I'm about to die, make it look like a murder. That way, my reputation won't be ruined by the drugs."

"Don't be stupid."

"Tell my son and father-in-law that-"

He died right on the spot, and I screamed. That prompted one person to run to the room where I was. The man that ran to the room me and Teal were in was quite shocked, I guess. I begged him to keep quiet as I told him about what had just happened. I offered him a lot of money to help me stage a murder scene, which he surprisingly accepted.

We agreed to a ruse; I would scream and run out crying that Teal was murdered. It worked, which was the end of that until Three came up with cocaine on their shirt and had bags on them. When the police came, Three snitched and made it complicated, so I had to play dumb about Teal's drug trade. I was good to go, but I felt guilty, especially for Nicky. I couldn't sleep, and I started taking pills to get over it.

I had started getting death threats from Teal's crew, who thought I snitched as well, so I had to disguise myself. A few days later, Detective Ryans called and told me I had to go to the confinement center for questioning and protection. The man who helped me staged Teal's death was also required to come as well. The day before questioning, we talked, and he stated he had started feeling guilty and might come clean. Of course, I was against it, but he was dead set on telling Officer Ryans the truth.

I stormed off, but not before angrily slipping him a warning. That was stupid of me because when I entered the center, he came afterward, letting me see a peek of the letter I wrote to him. I did what had to be done; while walking to the commons area, he went to the bathroom, and I followed him in. The moment he turned around, I punched his neck, and he went down. He was gasping for air, and I was freaked out, so I ran back to the commons area just in time for introductions. To lay low and avoid suspicion, I went to sleep. Well, I was gonna sleep anyway because of the pills, but you get what I mean. I forgot to take the note out, and somehow that led to the way things turned out right now.

Present

"What the hell?" questioned Three. "You killed Eight?"

"Accidently," said Seven. "But yeah, I was planning on it anyway."

"So Teal really was sick?" asked Five.

"Yes, he had an unknown disease, but the medicine you prescribed to him helped him. You didn't kill him; you actually prolonged his life. I know I don't speak for him, but on his behalf, thank you."

Five cried.

"I thought this would give you some closure," said Detective Ryans.

"Thank you," wept Five.

"I'll be leaving now. I wish you all the best."

"You too," replied Nine.

Detective Ryans left along with Seven and the other officer, shutting the door behind them. Five left shortly after as well.

"Well ain't that some bullshit." said Three.

"What do you mean?" asked Nine.

"This whole thing was for nothing. Even this number calling thing was useless."

"Not really. If you identify Teal Robertson as zero, then you have the answer."

"Huh?"

"Zero eliminated zero, making it a numeral paradox."

"Shut the f-

THE END

ABOUT THE AUTHOR

Albert Cooper is an 18 year old man. He likes to make music, watch anime and read comic books in his spare time. Currently, attending Georgia Highlands College Albert is studying for an English degree.